ISBN 978-0-545-42554-4

Text copyright © 2012 by Boxer Books Limited. Written by Paul Harrison.
Illustrations copyright © 2012 by Tom Knight.

12 11 10 9 8 7 6 5 4 3 2 1   12 13 14 15 16 17/0

Printed in the U.S.A.   40

First Scholastic printing, September 2012

The display type was set in Adobe Garamond.
The text type was set in Blackmoor Plain and Adobe Casion.

DR.ROACH'S MONSTROUS STORIES

NIGHT OF THE ZOMBIE GOLDFISH

SCHOLASTIC INC.

Contents

Dr. Roach Welcomes YOU!

Meet Judd Crank and his friend Zak. Two ordinary boys, in an ordinary town, with some very ordinary goldfish.

Who would have thought that those little goldfish would become great monsters and step right out of their tank and into town — looking for trouble!

How you ask? Come closer, my friend, and I'll tell you all about it.

Welcome to Dr. Roach's Monstrous Stories. Enjoy!

Dr. Roach

Chapter 1
Erupto-fizz

KABBOOOOFFFF!

Judd Crank peered at the results of his latest experiment through a cloud of thick purple smoke. Things hadn't gone exactly as planned.

"Hmm, perhaps just the one spoonful of pepper next time," Judd muttered to himself.

Judd loved chemistry. He loved the powders and potions and beakers and tubes. He loved it all so much he had managed to get his mom and dad to let him make a laboratory in the garage. Judd would spend hours there mixing, dabbling, and experimenting.

Judd kept a large tank full of goldfish next to his workbench. Judd loved his fish as much as he loved chemistry. He liked their color and the feeling of calm they gave him. He could watch his fish for hours.

He wasn't thinking of his fish right then, though. He was thinking about how to make his experiment, Erupto-fizz, work properly. But what he should have been thinking about was getting ready.

"Judd, are you ready yet?" his mother shouted from the house.

Judd took off his safety glasses, revealing two white circles in the purple soot around his panic-filled eyes. Was he ready yet? Ready for what? Suddenly, he remembered! He was going to Grandma's!

"Erm, yep, nearly, Mom. I'm just getting my stuff together," he fibbed.

"Judd, we're waiting for you. I hope you're not experimenting in there?"

Quickly, Judd scraped together the remains of the experiment and emptied them into the first empty container he could find — an empty fish-food can.

Judd stuffed the tin on a shelf and dashed out the garage.

"Coming, Mom!"

Chapter 2
Fishy, Fishy Flakes

Zak Pietersen was Judd's next-door neighbor and most trusted friend. He was the only person Judd would allow to look after his fish. Zak took his fish-feeding duties very seriously and, as usual, arrived nice and early the next day. He knew finding the fish food could take awhile.

Judd's laboratory was always a mess, and today was no different. If anything, it was worse. It looked as if a giant raccoon had broken in and pulled the place apart to find something tasty to eat. Zak sighed, but then he saw it. Right there on the shelf was a can of:

SOMETHING FISHY FISH FLAKES:
The favorite food of fish.

Nice one, Judd, he thought.

Happily Zak unscrewed the lid and tapped out some of the contents into the tank and then went over to Judd's workbench to look at Judd's latest experiment. Zak could never make heads or tails of what Judd was doing, but it all looked very exciting.

BURP!

"Excuse you," said Zak to the person who had belched. Then Zak realized — there was no one else!

BURP!

Zak spun around in a panic — who was making that noise?

BURP! It was the fish tank! It looked like a shaken soda bottle.

Huge bubbles of gas shot to the surface of the water, then exploded in belches, sending clouds of purple smoke billowing across the laboratory.

In a panic, Zak checked the label on the tin. There it was, clear as day: *Something Fishy Fish Flakes: The favorite food of fish*. It had to be the fish food, right?

The water inside the fish tank began to change color. It went green, then bright red, then electric blue, then yellow, then purple.

FIZZZZZZZZZZ!

WHIZZ! BANG!

Sparks began to shoot into the air, slopping the water all over the floor. The purple smoke swirled thicker and thicker over the edges of the tank, changing color with the water below. Zak turned around and ran for it.

Chapter 3
Zombie Goldfish

Zak thought that he had killed Judd's fish, but this wasn't true. The good news was that the fish were still alive. The bad news — no, sorry — the very bad news was that the chemicals Zak had tipped into the tank were actually changing Judd's beautiful, peaceful pets into . . .

ZOMBIE GOLDFISH.

There are three things you need to know about zombie goldfish:
1. They are really dumb.
2. Being zombies, they can live on land and walk on their flippers.
3. They are BIG.

As night fell, the goldfish crawled out of the purple, smoky water of the tank, slowly climbing on top of one another like a big, slippery, fishy pyramid.

They slid over the edge of the tank and onto the garage floor, where they lay getting bigger and bigger. Finally, they hauled their bodies upright, shuffled to the door — and broke their way through.

They were heading for town, and they were

HUNGRY!

Chapter 4
The Happy Haddock

Carp Creek, the town where Judd and Zak lived, was as quiet and sleepy a town as a quiet and sleepy town could ever be — until now.

The zombie goldfish were coming to town.

The Happy Haddock was Carp Creek's only restaurant. People wore their nicest clothes and everyone was on their best behavior. It was the last place you would expect to see a line of giant goldfish waddling through the door.

The head-
waiter, who
obviously
needed better
glasses, approached the zombies.

"I'm sorry," he said, "I'm afraid I can't allow you in without a tie."

The zombie at the front looked at the waiter for a moment with his big fishy eyes and then tried stuffing the waiter's head into his mouth.

"Euurrrgghhh!" cried the disgusted waiter as he pulled away. "Slimy!"

Fish was no longer on the menu at the Happy Haddock — the customers were!

The zombie goldfish attacked anything and everything to see if it was food. They nibbled napkins, chomped on chairs, gnawed people's knees, and bit their bottoms. Customers and waiters shrieked and screamed and stampeded for the door.

The word was out — the zombie goldfish were in town.

Next it was Carp Creek's fishing store — Hook, Line, and Sinker — that got a visit from the gruesome goldfish. The unfortunate customers discovered that the hunters had become

the hunted, as the fish
chased the fishermen.
Rods, reels, and fishing
lines went clattering to
the floor as the fearful
fishermen escaped out
the back door.

The townspeople
began to panic!

Chapter 5
Return to Carp Creek

When Judd and his parents returned to Carp Creek, they soon discovered that something very fishy was happening. There was a police roadblock and

some odd stories of giant fish. There were more nasty surprises for Judd at home, too.

"My goldfish are gone!" cried Judd, running out of the laboratory.

"Perhaps they got fed up with the mess and left," his dad joked.

"No — the door's been broken down and there's water all over the floor!"

"Honey, no one in Carp Creek would have stolen your fish," his mom reassured him. "Zak will know what happened."

Judd dashed straight to Zak's. He thought about the strange stories of giant fish he'd been hearing. There was no way the two could be connected, right?

Finally, he arrived.

"Hi, Mrs. Pietersen," said Judd after Zak's mom opened the door. "Is Zak home?"

"Sure, he's out back," she replied.

Judd sped past her and into the backyard. There was no one there.

"Zak!" Judd called.

There was no reply.

Then Judd heard a creaking sound from Zak's tree house. Judd looked up — just in time to see Zak duck away from the window.

Puzzled, Judd climbed the ladder to the tree house. Zak was there looking guilty.

"Sorry for killing your goldfish," said Zak quickly.

"You killed them?" said Judd.

"Yeah — I put the food in and the water went all bubbly and purple. Sorry."

"The food under the counter turned the water bubbly and purple?" said Judd.

"No, the food on the shelf next to the tank," Zak replied.

"Next to the tank . . . oh!" Judd realized what Zak had done. He'd put the remains of Judd's last experiment into the tank. "That wasn't food. That was my latest experiment — Erupto-fizz!"

Judd explained to Zak what had happened — but it still didn't explain why there were no goldfish floating in the water.

Unless . . .

"That's it! Those gigantic fish — they're mine!"

"What are you talking about?" said Zak.

"The powder must have changed them! And it's up to us to change them back!"

Judd jumped up.

"Where are you going?" asked Zak.

"To the lab to make the antidote. C'mon, I'm going to need your help."

Chapter 6
The Trap

The boys raced straight to Judd's laboratory.

"So if you're making the antidote, what do I do?" Zak asked.

"I'm going to need you to attract the fish."

"Attract the fish?" Zak repeated.

"You're going to lead them into our trap."

"We've got a trap?" asked Zak.

"Not yet — but we will."

Judd started pulling paper, pens, and wire out from some boxes in one corner of the garage.

"Here we are," said Judd.

"We're going to trap them with arts and crafts?" asked Zak.

"No, it's your costume," Judd replied. "You need to put it on to lure the fish."

"No way!" said Zak. "Not a chance! No, no, nopey no."

Ten minutes later, Zak was dressed as a large can of Something Fishy Fish Flakes: the favorite food of fish.

"I look ridiculous," Zak grumbled as Judd helped him into the costume.

"You look great — anyway, it's all part of the plan," said Judd. "They're hungry, so they'll follow you."

"They're going to eat me?!" Zak exclaimed.

"Not if you're quick," replied
Judd cheerfully. "Now go find
my fish — I've got chemistry to
do. I'll call your cell phone
when I'm done."

Zak tripped over in his
costume for the twentieth
time and lay on the ground
complaining.

   "This is a crazy idea,"

he grumbled. "I wish I *had* killed his dumb fish. How am I supposed to run dressed as a giant can of fish food? And where am I supposed to find those fish anyway?"

Zak struggled to his feet and turned to go home.

There, staring at him with big, dead eyes, were fifteen zombie goldfish. "Oh," said Zak. "There they are."

Chapter 7
The Chase

"Aaaaaaaaaaaaaaaaaaaaaaaaaaaaaaaarrrr
rrrrrrrrgggghhhhhh!" Zak screamed.
He was running down the sidewalk
as fast as his feet could carry him.
Unfortunately, this wasn't quite quick
enough. Zak's costume stopped him
from taking big steps, so the zombie

goldfish were right behind him —
and gaining fast!

**BIDDLY-DEE BIDDLY-DOO,
BIDDLY-DEE BIDDLY-DOO,
WOOP-WOOP, BIDDLY-DEE
BIDDLY-DOO . . .**

Zak fumbled with the costume and
took out his cell phone.

BIDDLY-DEE BIDDLY-DOO, WOOP-WOO...

"Hi," gasped Zak. "Sorry but this really isn't a great time. . . ."

"Zak, it's me, Judd — don't hang up!" said the voice on the phone. "Have you found the fish yet?"

"Well, they kind of found me," Zak replied.

"Great. Can you get them to follow you?" asked Judd.

"Oh, yeah," said Zak. "That part of the plan is going too well, if anything."

Behind him the zombie goldfish were getting closer.

"Great," said Judd. "Are you running? You sound out of breath. Never mind. Bring the fish to the swimming pool — I'll be waiting there."

"Can't you come to me?" pleaded Zak, but Judd had already hung up.

The zombies were so close that Zak could almost feel their fishy breath, but Carp Creek's outdoor pool was just around the corner. Behind him, Zak could hear the **SLAP SLAP SLAP** of the zombies' tail fins as they pounded the sidewalk.

Zak barged through the entry gates with the goldfish in hot pursuit.

"Judd!" Zak called, looking wildly from side to side as he ran, but it was difficult to see through the narrow eye slit of his costume. Suddenly, the ground started to feel bouncy. Zak looked down — he was standing at the end of the diving board, wobbling

over the water. Carefully, he turned around to get off, but there, shuffling along the board toward him, were the zombie goldfish!

Chapter 8
Celebration Time

"Zak — jump!"
    It was Judd,
standing by the edge
of the pool. Zak
didn't think twice.
Splash!

The zombies shuffled to the end of the board. With fifteen more splashes, they followed Zak into the pool. By then, Judd was already fishing Zak out of the water.

Zak sat on the side, coughing and spluttering inside his soggy costume. Judd emptied a large bucket full of his antidote into the pool.

Nothing happened. Then . . .

BURP!

The water began to steam and boil. Great bubbles began to rise and belched out green clouds of smoke. The water changed color from purple, to yellow, to electric blue, to bright red, then green. The belching got louder and the smoke got thicker, until neither Judd nor Zak could see. Suddenly, there was a massive, final BUUURRRRPPPPP! and the boys were showered with a watery green slime.

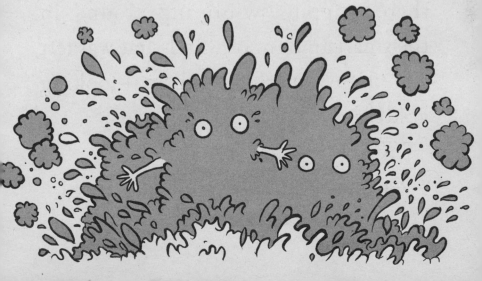

Eventually the smoke cleared. Most of the water that had been in the swimming pool was now out of the pool. But there, happily swimming around in the small amount of water that was left were fifteen perfectly normal-looking goldfish.

"We've done it!" cried Judd.

Zak did not reply. He had fainted.

There was, of course, a big celebration in Carp Creek. The mayor made a long speech, the town band played some terrible music, and the local paper took some bad photographs. While the crowd applauded, Judd leaned over to Zak.

"Cheer up, you're a hero," he said.

"Oh, sure. You did all the smart stuff. I just dressed up as fish food and got chased

across town by giant goldfish. Some hero," Zak replied.

"Yeah, but if you hadn't done that, I wouldn't have been able to make the antidote. We're a team."

Zak smiled. "Yeah, I guess so. Only one thing: don't ever ask me to feed your goldfish again."

Judd laughed. "Seriously though,

what are the chances of that ever happening again?" he asked.

Across town, in Judd's laboratory, all was quiet — messy, but quiet. In a tank swam fifteen happy normal goldfish. Normal that is, apart from the wings that they were beginning to sprout from their backs . . .

DR. ROACH'S
MONSTROUS STORIES

ATTACK OF THE
GIANT
HAMSTER

HURRY!

Have you seen those ads that say they will make you beautiful and slim, give you big muscles and even more hair? Pish posh I say — it's all make-believe. Or is it?

Our story is about Hercules. No, not the mighty Greek hero — but a pet hamster called Hercules. He isn't strong. He is a small, fluffy, lazy, hamstery slob.

How amazing, then, that Hercules is able to scare the townsfolk, crush cars, and trample the farmers' market in search of some delicious food!

How you ask? Get a copy today and I'll tell you everything!

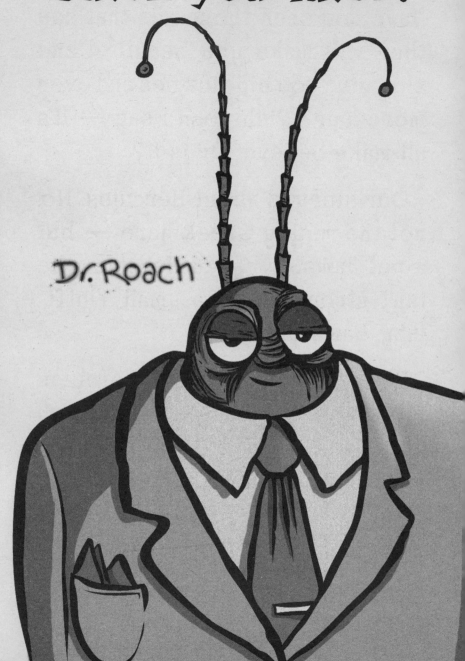